A Small Kindness

by **Stacy McAnulty**

Illustrated by **Wendy Leach**

RP|KIDS
PHILADELPHIA

Running Press Kids
Hachette Book Group
1290 Avenue of the Americas, New York, NY 10104
www.runningpress.com/rpkids
@RP_Kids

Printed in China

First Edition: February 2021

Published by Running Press Kids, an imprint of Perseus Books, LLC,
a subsidiary of Hachette Book Group, Inc. The Running Press Kids name
and logo is a trademark of the Hachette Book Group.

The Hachette Speakers Bureau provides a wide range of authors for
speaking events. To find out more, go to www.hachettespeakersbureau.
com or call (866) 376-6591.

The publisher is not responsible for websites (or their content)
that are not owned by the publisher.

Print book cover and interior design by Frances J. Soo Ping Chow.

Library of Congress Control Number: 2019946934

ISBNs: 978-0-7624-9522-1 (hardcover), 978-0-7624-9523-8 (ebook),
978-0-7624-7013-6 (ebook), 978-0-7624-7012-9 (ebook)

APS

10 9 8 7 6 5 4 3 2 1

For Suzanne—SJM

For Wesley—WL

It was like a game of tag.

Alice smiled at Lucas.

Lucas said hello to Jasmine.

Jasmine gave a turn
to Xavier.

Xavier held the door
for Ms. Jones.

Ms. Jones made Henry laugh.

Henry complimented Cora.

Cora offered a seat to Mateo.

Mateo listened to Isaiah.

Isaiah lent a hand to Mr. Freeman.

Mr. Freeman encouraged Rhea.

Rhea wrote a note to Lily.

Lily shared with Declan.

Declan high-fived Alice.

It was like a game of tag.

And everybody won.

DATE DUE			